SIMON PUTTOCK was born in New Zealand, and travelled
all over the world as a child. He has had a varied career,
from cinema projectionist, to sound engineer to singer/songwriter
and cabaret club disc jockey. He has worked for Waterstone's Newcastle
for nine years, and now runs the Children's Department.
Simon's previous titles include *Coral Goes Swimming* (Hodder),
Here I Am! Said Smedley (Egmont) and to come,
A Story for Hippo (Egmont).

ALISON JAY specialised in illustration at the London College
of Printing, where she gained a 1st Class Honours degree.
Her previous titles include *Emma's Doll* by Brian Patten (Penguin),
The Lion Treasury of Children's Prayers (Lion), *Picture This* (Templar)
and *The Dream Pack* (Duncan Baird).

For Vivian French, with love — S.P.
For Jack and Penny — A.J.

First published in Great Britain in 2001 by
Frances Lincoln Limited, 4 Torriano Mews,
Torriano Avenue, London NW5 2RZ

First paperback edition 2002

British Library Cataloguing in Publication Data available on request

0-7112-1575-8 hardback
0-7112-1825-0 paperback

Printed in Singapore

1 3 5 7 9 8 6 4 2

A Ladder to the Stars

Simon Puttock
Illustrated by Alison Jay

FRANCES LINCOLN

It was a little girl's birthday. She was seven years old. From her bedroom window, she looked out and saw a single star dancing in the velvet blue. It glittered and span so beautifully, she wished she could climb right up into the sky and dance along with it.

"Twinkle twinkle, little star. How I wonder what you are.
I wish I may, I wish I might, have the wish I wish tonight."

The star heard the little girl and began to show off, whirling
and dipping as never before.

   When the moon rose, it saw the star capering and was curious.

   "What are you doing, little star?"

   The star turned catherine wheels and told the moon about
the little girl's wish.

The moon grew round and full pondering the matter,
then wasted away to a splinter worrying about what to do.
   "I must tell the sun," the moon decided, "for the sun is also
a star and loves all things that love to dance."

The sun called the wind and the clouds and the weather together, and they thought up a plan.

The wind set out to find a special seed. It whistled away to billow and blow through every nook and cranny of the planet.

At last, worn down to the breath of a breeze, the wind found the special seed and blew it gently back to the little girl's garden and planted it in a dusty corner.

Soon, the seed sent a root into the soil.
It pushed up a slender stem, and spread
leaves to the light of the waiting sun.

It grew ...   and grew ...

and grew ...   and grew ...

and did not stop growing until ...

... one day it had grown so high, the tips of its branches
brushed the belly of the sky.

When its leaves tickled the sun as it passed overhead,
the sun told the moon to tell the star to tell the little girl
that her wish had been granted.

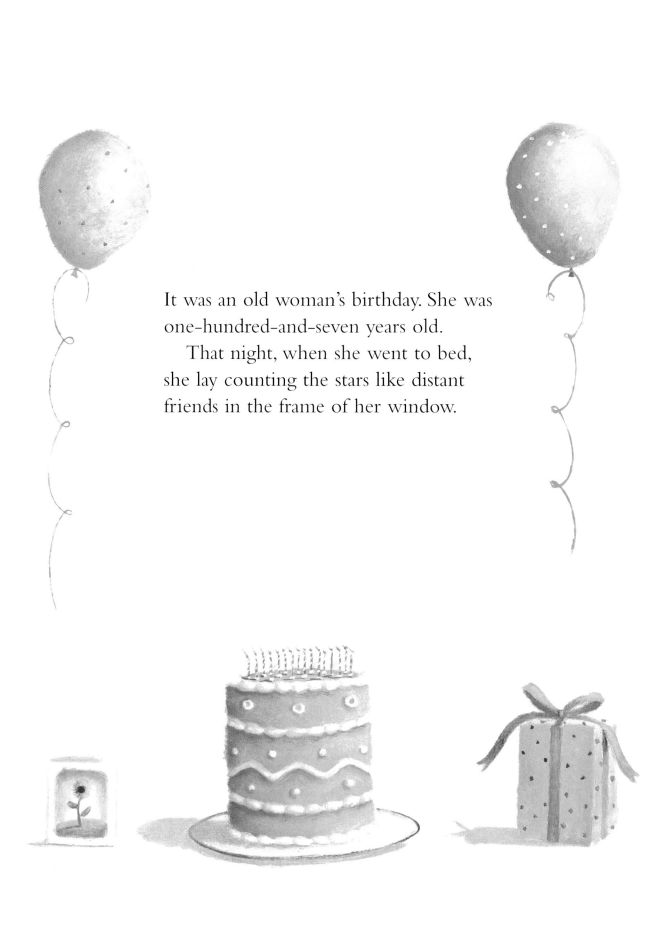

It was an old woman's birthday. She was one-hundred-and-seven years old.

That night, when she went to bed, she lay counting the stars like distant friends in the frame of her window.

But a single, piercing beam of starlight shone in and would not let her sleep.

"Hey, little girl!"

The old woman rubbed her eyes and looked up at the sky.

"Who, me?"

"Yes, you," said the star.

"I'm not a little girl. I'm an old woman, and I'm tired. Now go away and let me sleep."

"Come out and climb the tree. Come up and dance," the star entreated. "It was your wish."

"Are you crazy?" cried the old woman. "That must have been a hundred years ago. I am too old and it is too late now to climb to the top of that great, tall tree."

"It is never too late," said the star. "Why, one hundred years are nothing and no time. To a star, they are light and quick like seeds in the wind. You are still a little girl to us and we are waiting for you. Please come."

The old woman, whose life had been long and whose bones were weary, remembered how it felt to be young and carefree. She remembered, too, a birthday long ago when the sky had seemed vast and mysterious. Above her the stars winked and beckoned.

"I will," she said at last, "I WILL!"

And despite her aching back and trembling limbs, she fetched
a chair to stand on, rubbed her hands on the bark for luck
and began to climb.

It was breathless, hot, hard work. The old woman felt inclined to grumble as she climbed, while below her the city lights sparkled like another sky of stars.

"Twinkle twinkle, silly star. How I wish you weren't so far."

But as she climbed higher, the air grew cooler and clearer
and the climbing easier, until she was so high up that
the world was lost in the clouds beneath her feet.
She was climbing so fast, that when
she reached the top she bumped
her head hard up against
the belly of midnight.
     "Ouch!"

She rubbed her head and eyed the sky an inch above
her nose, as branches swayed beneath her feet.
"Goodbye, goodbye," she told the tree.
"All those years I sat in your shade
and watched you grow,
but I never knew
you grew for me.
Thank you."

Then she spat on her hands for strength, and with a mighty effort, pushed and pulled and wriggled and heaved her way though the satin skin of the sky.

   "Oh my! Oh my! How elegant you are," she said to the stars. "You twinkle like diamonds."

"Thank you," said her special star. "Shall we dance at last?"
The old woman smiled and held out her hands, and they kicked
up their heels till a million sparks like new-born comets flew,
and off they span away across the endless, velvet blue.

All this was a long, long time ago, but when you
are dancing with stars, the years are little and quick
like seeds in the wind.

She is dancing still.

MORE PICTURE BOOKS IN PAPERBACK
FROM FRANCES LINCOLN

The Egg
Mark Robertson

When George discovers a rather large egg under his mother's favourite
chicken, he soon finds himself looking after a baby dragon.
But the dragon soon begins pining for his own kind,
and one day he disappears...

Suitable for National Curriculum English – Reading, Key Stages 1 and 2
Scottish Guidelines English Language – Reading, Levels A, B and C;
Religious and Moral Education, Levels A and B.

0-7112-1525-1   £5.99

The Star Bearer
Dianne Hofmeyr
Illustrated by Jude Daly

Dianne Hofmeyr's retelling of a 5,000-year-old Ancient Egyptian
creation myth, finely illustrated by Jude Daly, gives an enchanting explanation
of how our starry universe came to be.

Suitable for National Curriculum English – Reading, Key Stage 2; History, Key Stage 2
Scottish Guidelines English Language – Reading, Levels B and C

0-7112-1663-0   £5.99

Fair, Brown and Trembling
Jude Daly

Jude Daly's retelling of this lively Irish folk tale,
illustrated with delightful characters and velvet landscapes,
has its roots deep in the Cinderella story.

Suitable for National Curriculum English – Reading, Key Stages 1 and 2.
Scottish Guidelines English Language – Reading, Level B

0-7112-1462-X   £5.99

Frances Lincoln titles are available from all good bookshops.
Prices are correct at time of publication, but may be subject to change.